leapfrog

Dick Whittington

First published in 2005 by
Franklin Watts
96 Leonard Street
London
EC2A 4XD

Franklin Watts Australia
Level 17/207 Kent Street
Sydney
NSW 2000

A CIP catalogue record for this book is available
from the British Library.

ISBN 0 7496 6158 5 (hbk)
ISBN 0 7496 6170 4 (pbk)

Series Editor: Jackie Hamley
Series Advisor: Dr Barrie Wade
Series Designer: Peter Scoulding

Printed in China

Dick Whittington

Retold by Margaret Nash

Illustrated by Martin Remphry

W
FRANKLIN WATTS
LONDON·SYDNEY

Long, long ago, there
lived a poor boy called
Dick Whittington.

People told Dick that the streets of London were paved with gold.

He set off to seek his
fortune there.

But when Dick reached London, the streets were dirty.

Dick was tired and hungry.
He fell asleep outside a
rich merchant's house.

Next day, the merchant
and his daughter, Alice,
found Dick. "You poor
boy!" said the merchant.

"You can live here and work in my kitchen, if you want."

Dick worked hard for the merchant, even though the cook kept telling him off.

There were rats in his bedroom, too. Dick bought a cat to get rid of them.

One day, the merchant began loading his ship with goods to sell in far-off lands.

"They will make my fortune," he told his servants. "I will sell things for you, too, if you wish."

Everyone gave something
to sell. Dick only had his
cat so, sadly, he gave her.

"Don't worry. She'll be all right," said Alice. She and Dick became good friends.

No matter how hard Dick worked, the cook still told him off. She beat him, too.

Dick was so unhappy that,
one day, he ran away.

Dick walked to the edge of London. When he sat down, he heard church bells ringing loudly.

"Turn again, Whittington,
Lord Mayor of London.
Turn again, Whittington!"
they seemed to say.

Dick stood up. He turned.

Then he hurried back to the house.

The merchant was back home. He greeted Dick happily and gave him a big bag of gold.

"This is all yours, Dick!" he said. "The King of Barbary paid highly for your cat to get rid of the rats in his palace."

Dick gasped with joy.

He had made his fortune!

"Well done!" said Alice.

"You deserve it!"

Later on, Dick married Alice. He also became the Lord Mayor of London, just as the bells said he would!

Leapfrog has been specially designed to fit the requirements of the National Literacy Strategy. It offers real books for beginning readers by top authors and illustrators.

There are 37 Leapfrog stories to choose from:

The Bossy Cockerel
ISBN 0 7496 3828 1

Bill's Baggy Trousers
ISBN 0 7496 3829 X

Mr Spotty's Potty
ISBN 0 7496 3831 1

Little Joe's Big Race
ISBN 0 7496 3832 X

The Little Star
ISBN 0 7496 3833 8

The Cheeky Monkey
ISBN 0 7496 3830 3

Selfish Sophie
ISBN 0 7496 4385 4

Recycled!
ISBN 0 7496 4388 9

Felix on the Move
ISBN 0 7496 4387 0

Pippa and Poppa
ISBN 0 7496 4386 2

Jack's Party
ISBN 0 7496 4389 7

The Best Snowman
ISBN 0 7496 4390 0

Eight Enormous Elephants
ISBN 0 7496 4634 9

Mary and the Fairy
ISBN 0 7496 4633 0

The Crying Princess
ISBN 0 7496 4632 2

Jasper and Jess
ISBN 0 7496 4081 2

The Lazy Scarecrow
ISBN 0 7496 4082 0

The Naughty Puppy
ISBN 0 7496 4383 8

Freddie's Fears
ISBN 0 7496 4382 X

Cinderella
ISBN 0 7496 4228 9

The Three Little Pigs
ISBN 0 7496 4227 0

Jack and the Beanstalk
ISBN 0 7496 4229 7

The Three Billy Goats Gruff
ISBN 0 7496 4226 2

Goldilocks and the Three Bears
ISBN 0 7496 4225 4

Little Red Riding Hood
ISBN 0 7496 4224 6

Rapunzel
ISBN 0 7496 6147 X*
ISBN 0 7496 6159 3

Snow White
ISBN 0 7496 6149 6*
ISBN 0 7496 6161 5

The Emperor's New Clothes
ISBN 0 7496 6151 8*
ISBN 0 7496 6163 1

The Pied Piper of Hamelin
ISBN 0 7496 6152 6*
ISBN 0 7496 6164 X

Hansel and Gretel
ISBN 0 7496 6150 X*
ISBN 0 7496 6162 3

The Sleeping Beauty
ISBN 0 7496 6148 8*
ISBN 0 7496 6160 7

Rumpelstiltskin
ISBN 0 7496 6153 4*
ISBN 0 7496 6165 8

The Ugly Duckling
ISBN 0 7496 6154 2*
ISBN 0 7496 6166 6

Puss in Boots
ISBN 0 7496 6155 0*
ISBN 0 7496 6167 4

The Frog Prince
ISBN 0 7496 6156 9*
ISBN 0 7496 6168 2

The Princess and the Pea
ISBN 0 7496 6157 7*
ISBN 0 7496 6169 0

Dick Whittington
ISBN 0 7496 6158 5*
ISBN 0 7496 6170 4

* hardback